Congrats on graduating Sherry!! Best of luck to you. We know you will do great things.

Love,
Jon, Amber & Logan

CONGRATULATIONS!

To:

From:

Yay, Keith!

Published by Simon & Schuster
1230 Avenue of the Americas, New York, New York 10020
© 2001 by Sandra Boynton. All rights reserved including the right of reproduction in whole or in part in any form.
Printed in the United States of America
6 8 10 9 7
Library of Congress Cataloging-in-Publication Data
Boynton, Sandra.
Yay, You! moving out, moving up, moving on / by Sandra Boynton. 1st ed.
p. cm.
Summary: In rhyme, outlines some of the possibilities
that life has to offer, from the adventurous to the tranquil.
ISBN 0-689-84283-X
[1. Individuality—Fiction. 2. Stories in rhyme.] I. Title.
PZ8.3.B7Yay 2001   [E]—dc21   00-063509

and **THANKYOUTHANKYOUTHANKYOU**, *Caitlin!*

YAY, YOU!

Moving Out,
Moving Up,
Moving On

Written and Illustrated by
Sandra Boynton

Simon & Schuster

New York   London   Toronto   Sydney   Singapore

Yay, you!

You did it!
You're done!
You made it!
You're through!

4

OH, WHAT A GREAT MOMENT!

Now what will you do?

There are so many choices.
The world is immense.
Take a good look around
and decide what makes sense.

Some like to go fast.

Some like to go slow.

Some like to get going
however they go.

Some strive to be peaceful,
and joyful, and wise.

OOM.

Some
choose
to just
ponder
the size
of their
thighs.

11

So look north!

And look south!

Look ahead!

Look behind!

12

Should you live where it's cold?

Should
you live
where
it's hot?

15

Do you want to be terribly busy?

Or not?

Do you need lots of friends,

or only a few?

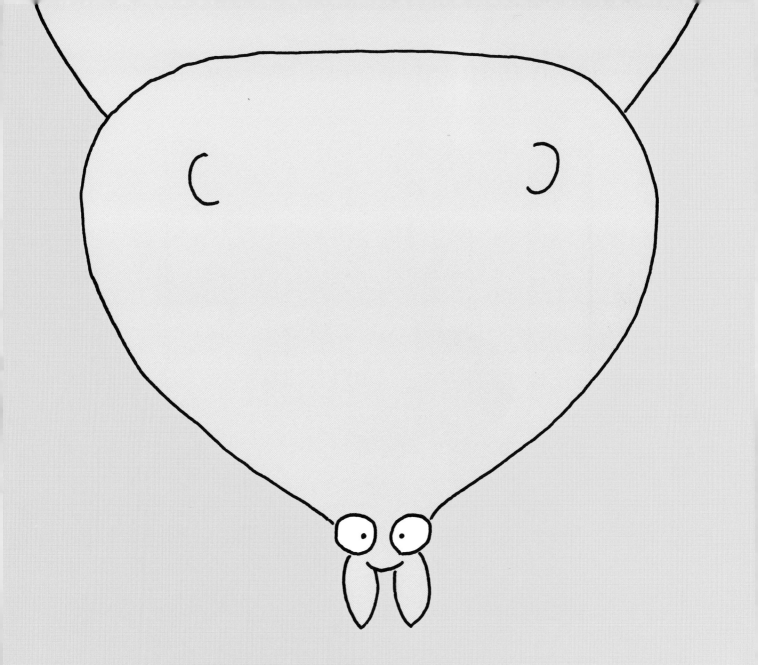

Would you like to have friends
with a new point of view?

Is your mind moved by science?

Or does
art
move your soul?

Do you listen
to rivers,

or to great rock-and-roll?

Do you long for adventure?
Do you love to read maps?

Would you rather stay home
with your chocolate,
perhaps?

You already have wit.
You already have style.

You have very kind eyes
and a dazzling smile.

Hey!
What's the hurry,
anyhow?

There are **PLACES TO GET TO!**

And **PROJECTS TO DO!**

PEOPLE TO TALK WITH, and **LUNCHES TO CHEW!**

29

But stopping a while
is okay, too.

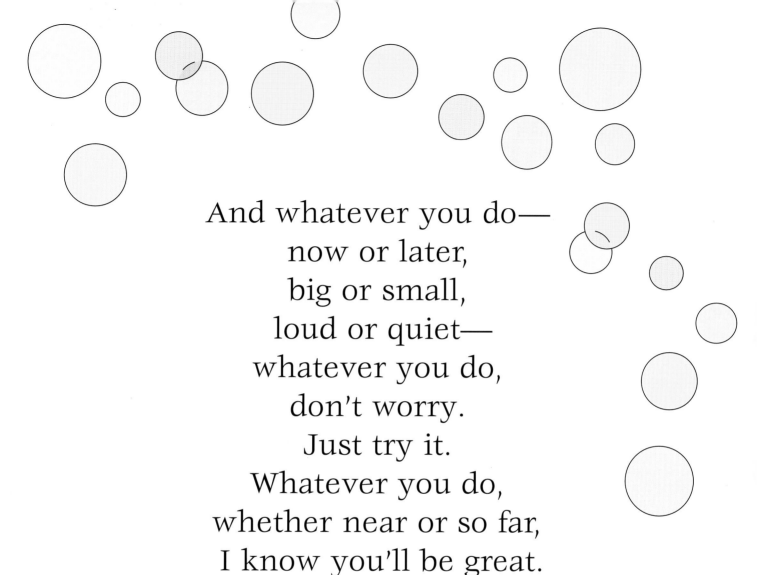

And whatever you do—
now or later,
big or small,
loud or quiet—
whatever you do,
don't worry.
Just try it.
Whatever you do,
whether near or so far,
I know you'll be great.

You already are.